FARMER JOE
and the
MUSIC SHOW

To Alice Blacker, The Old Crow Medicine Show,
and The Hot Bang – T.M.

For Dylan,
with special thanks to Liz Johnson and Tim Rose,
for their wit and wisdom – G.P.-R.

ISBN: 978-0-545-23324-8

Text copyright © 2008 by Tony Mitton.
Illustrations copyright © 2008 by Guy Parker-Rees.
All rights reserved. Published by Orchard Books, an imprint of Scholastic Inc.
ORCHARD BOOKS and design are registered trademarks of Watts Publishing Group, Ltd.,
used under license. SCHOLASTIC and associated logos are trademarks
and/or registered trademarks of Scholastic Inc.

12 11 10 9 8 7 6 5 4 3 2 1   10 11 12 13 14 15/0

Printed in the U.S.A.   08

First Scholastic printing, January 2010

FARMER JOE
and the
MUSIC SHOW

By
Tony Mitton

Illustrations by
Guy Parker-Rees

SCHOLASTIC INC.
New York Toronto London Auckland
Sydney Mexico City New Delhi Hong Kong

Down on the farm of Poor Old Joe,
the hens won't lay and the crops won't grow.

The cows won't graze and the pigs won't feed,
and Joe just can't think what they need.

But suddenly Joe has a bright idea:
Music has the power to cheer!

He puts on his hat and yells, **"Yee-har!"**

Then he starts to pluck on his old guitar.

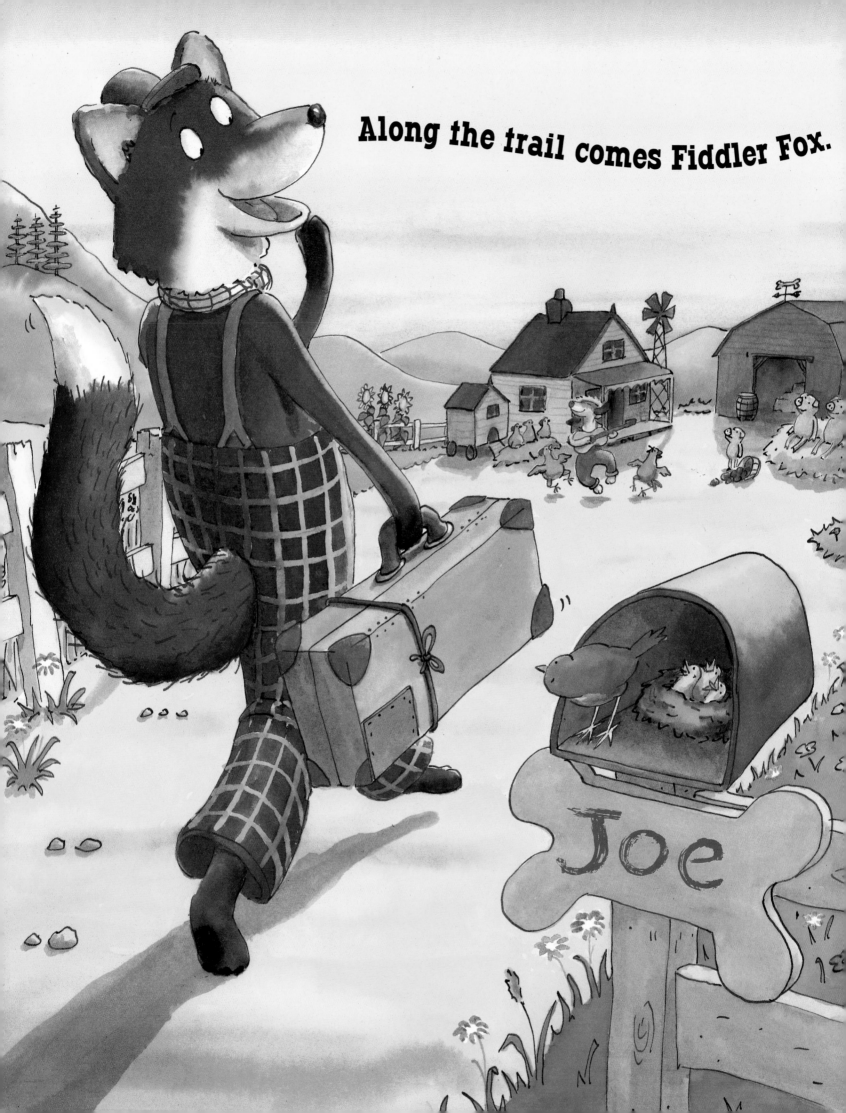

Along the trail comes Fiddler Fox.

He pulls out a fiddle from a battered old box.

He tunes the strings

and he lifts the bow,

playing it nifty, playing it neat,
till the pigs start dancing to the music's beat.

Out of a burrow pop two big ears.
Rabbit just loves that stuff she hears.

She hops from her hole and starts to play
on a concertina, right away!

Concertina, **wheee-hee-hah,**
skiddly fiddle and old guitar.
The crops like the music. Me-oh-my!
Look at them stretching up to the sky!

Now, what's that rumbling, grumbling sound?
Something **big** is stumbling round.

Soon we'll see it face to face . . .

Wow! It's Bear with a double bass!
Doom-doom-doo

and
**whoom-
whoom-
whum,**

Bear's bass booms with a deep, low thrum.

the bees go buzz as they hum around,
and Bear's bass booms as he stomps the ground.

The cows start mooing as the music plays,
then they click their hooves as they bend to graze.

The creatures caper — look at them go —
to the thrill of the hillbilly music show.

They **jump** and **jive.**
They **leap** and **bound.**
They love the rhythm of the country sound.

But now it's hot, and the sun rides high, and the heat beats down from the big, blue sky.

What'll they do now?
What do you think?
Sprawl in the shade with a nice, cool drink.

So down on the farm of Clever Old Joe,
the hens all lay and the crops all grow.
The cows all graze and the pigs all feed,
and Joe knows just the thing they need.